The Hopes and Dreams Series

Mexican-Americans

# The Magic Paper

A story based on history

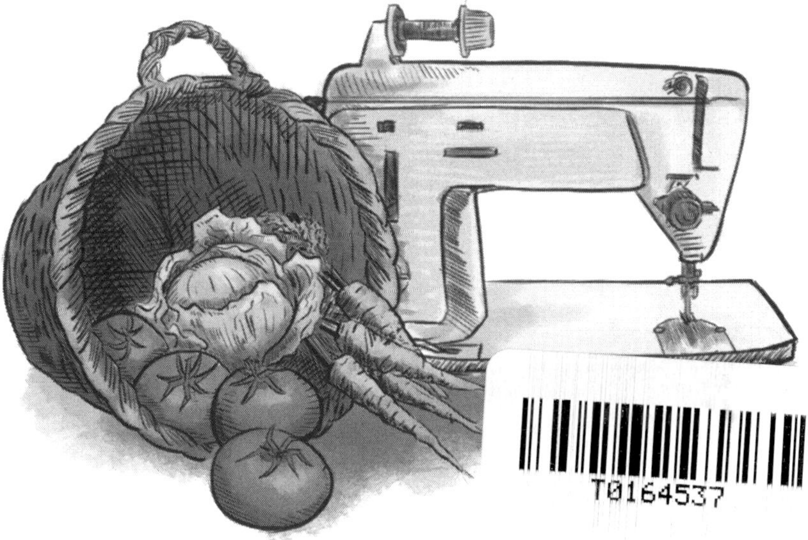



Second Edition

Tana Reiff

Illustrations by Tyler Stiene

PRO LINGUA LEARNING

# Pro Lingua Learning

PO Box 4467, Rockville, Maryland 20849
Office: 1-301-242-8900, Book orders: 1-800-888-4741
Web: ProLinguaLearning.com
Email: info@ProLinguaLearning.com

Print Edition ISBN 978-0-86647-383-5

The first edition of this book was originally published by Fearon Education, a division of David S. Lake Publishers, Belmont, California, Copyright © 1989, later by Pearson Education. This, the second edition, has been revised and redesigned.

The cover and illustrations are by Tyler Stiene. The book was set and designed by Tana Reiff, consulting with A.A. Burrows, using the Adobe *Century Schoolbook* typeface for the text. This is a digital adaptation of one of the most popular faces of the twentieth century. Century's distinctive roman and italic fonts and its clear, dark strokes and serifs were designed, as the name suggests, to make schoolbooks easy to read. The display font used on the cover and titles is a 21st-century digital invention titled Telugu. It is designed to work on all digital platforms and with Indic scripts. Telugu is named for the Telugu people in southern India and their widely spoken language. This is a simple, strong, and interesting sans serif display font.

**Audio MP3 files for this book are available for purchase and download at ProLinguaLearning.com/audio.**

## The Hopes and Dreams Series
by Tana Reiff

The Magic Paper (Mexican-Americans)
For Gold and Blood (Chinese-Americans)
Nobody Knows (African-Americans)
Little Italy (Italian-Americans)
Hungry No More (Irish-Americans)
Sent Away (Japanese-Americans)
Two Hearts (Greek-Americans)
A Different Home (Cuban-Americans)
The Family from Vietnam (Vietnamese-Americans)
Old Ways, New Ways (Jewish-Americans)
Amala's Hope (A Family from Syria)
Neighbors (A Family from El Salvador)

# Contents

# 1 The Visa

Mexico City, Mexico, 1980

The line of people
seemed a mile long.
It seemed
half of Mexico
wanted a visa today.
The line moved very slowly.

Teresa Garcia
had been here
since early morning.
Now it was 3:00
in the afternoon.
She was hungry.
Sometimes she sat
on the ground
to rest her feet.

Then someone
poked her.
She turned around.
"Need a visa?"
a young man asked her.

"That's why I'm here,"
Teresa said.
"I need to visit
my aunt and uncle.
They live in Los Angeles.
My aunt is sick.
I want
to take care of her.
I don't plan
to stay in the U.S.
My family is here
in Mexico City."

The young man
put his face
close to Teresa's ear.
"You will never
get a visa here,"
he whispered.
"Many people
are turned down.
But I can get you one.
Real fast."

"A real visa?"
Teresa asked.

"It will look real.
That's what matters,"
said the man.
"You give me
your pesos.
I'll bring your visa
in one hour."

Teresa walked away
from the long line.

The young man
led her around the corner.
He took her picture.
Then he took her money.

"I'll be back
in one hour,"
he said.
"You have my word."

Teresa waited.
She wasn't sure
she had done
the right thing.

What would happen
if the fake visa
didn't work?
Or what if the man
ran away
with her money?

But an hour later,
true to his word,
he came back.
He handed Teresa
her new visa.
"Have a great trip!"
he smiled.

The next day
Teresa said goodbye
to her family.
She walked
to the bus station.
She got on a bus
heading north.
Two days later,
the bus
pulled into Los Angeles.

## 2   Los Angeles

"Oh, Tia*!
I am so sorry you are sick.
Oh, but Los Angeles
is so nice!"
Teresa said to her aunt.
"Now I see
how very poor
the people in Mexico are!
Here, there are jobs.
People can eat
whenever they are hungry."

"This is true,"
said her aunt Silvia.
"We do not
run out of food.
We are far from rich.
But we are not
dirt poor either."

"Do you think
I could work
while I am here?"
asked Teresa.

*Tia means aunt in Spanish. Tio means uncle.

"After you
are feeling better?
I want to pay
for my own food.
And I would love
to send money home.
My family
really needs it."

    "You may not work,"
said Silvia.
"You do not have
the right kind of visa."

    Her uncle
was shaking his head.
"I can find you work,"
said Ruben.
"In a dress factory.
I know people there.
No one there
will check your visa."

    So, when Tia felt better,
Teresa went to work
in a dress factory.

She got paid in cash.
Not by the hour.
It was piece work.
She got paid
for each dress she sewed.
The faster she worked,
the more money
she made.
She worked
12 hours a day
to make more money.

One day,
Teresa's nose
began to run.
It must be a cold,
she told herself.
But days later,
her nose
was still running.
She felt hot
all the time.
She could not work.
She was sick,
but no work,
no pay.

"You are not well,
dear girl,"
said Silvia.
"The dress factory
made you sick.
The air in that place
can get pretty bad.
Now it is my turn
to take care of you."

"Tia, I have something
to tell you,"
Teresa began.
"I have already stayed
in the U.S.
too long.
My visa is no good now.
You are feeling better.
Maybe this would be
a good time for me
to go back to Mexico."

"You cannot go
when you are sick,"
said Silvia.
"You must stay here
until you feel better."

In a few days
Teresa felt better.
But she did not want
to leave Los Angeles.

Work was hard to find
back home.
She could never make
as much money
as she did
in the dress factory.
If she stayed here,
her family back home
would be better off.

"Stay with us
as long as you want,"
Ruben told her.
"Both Tia and I
have green cards.
We may live here
as long as we want.
But lots of people
live here without papers."

"I don't want Teresa
to get into trouble,"
said Silvia.

"What is the worst thing
that could happen?"
Ruben asked Silvia.
"They would send her
back to Mexico."

"Oh, thank you
for letting me stay,"
said Teresa.
"I will
take my chances.
I will stay
a little longer.
I will find
a new job.
But I'm afraid
I will not feel safe.
I will look
around every corner.
I will always be afraid
of getting caught."

## 3  Benito

Back in Mexico
there was a young man
named Benito Cruz.
He lived in a little village
out in the country.
Everyone there
was very poor.
There was not enough work
for all the people.
Women cooked
and took care of children.
Young men and old men
sat and talked
and played games
all day long.

Benito sat
with the other men.
"I have gone north
and back again
five or six times,"
he told them.

"I have gone
by bus,
by train,
by car,
by boat.
I have walked
part of the way.
I always come back
because this is home.
But there is no work here.
It was good
up in the U.S.
One hour's pay
in California
is the same as
one day's pay here."

"What will you do?"
an old man asked him.

"Go north again,"
said Benito.
"I can always get
farm work up there."

"One of these days
you will get caught
at the border,"
said the old man.

"I saved
some money
from my last trip,"
laughed Benito.
"I will get
across the border."

"I wish you luck,"
said the old man.

The next day,
Benito walked
to the main road.
He waited
for a ride.
Before long,
a truck stopped.

"I'll take you
close to the border,"
said the driver.
"You must cross over
by yourself."

But only a few miles
down the road,
a police officer
stopped the truck.

"Don't lie to me,"
said the officer.
"I know
where you're going.
No visa, right?"

Benito shook his head.

"I'll let you pass,"
said the officer.
"But first you must pay me.
Think of it
as a small fine
for breaking the law."

Benito gave the officer
some money.
The truck went on.

At the border,
Benito got out
of the truck.
"Good luck!"
the driver shouted.

Benito waited for help
to cross the border.
He walked around
until he found
a coyote.

"I need a ride
into California,"
Benito told the man.

"You know my price,"
said the coyote.
"But no rides today,
the border
is too hot.
Border patrol all over.

Can't get a bus
full of wetbacks
across today."

"I can't wait
till another day!"
said Benito.

So the coyote
showed Benito
a big pipe
that went under ground.

"This is your way
into the U.S. today, "
said the coyote.
"Just crawl inside
and keep going
to the end."

Benito did not move.

"Hurry up!"
said the man.
"If we stand here
they will catch us."

Benito did
what the coyote
told him to do.
He got down
on his hands and knees.
He crawled
into the pipe.
It was dark and wet.
The air smelled bad.
Benito crawled along
like a worm.

It was hard to move.
It was hard to breathe.
Benito tried
to raise his head
and hit the top
of the pipe.
He got scared.
What if he
couldn't make it
to the other end?
He felt something
crawling over his legs.
Could it be a rat?
Benito tried
to move faster.

At last,
he saw light
ahead of him.
He reached
the end of the pipe.
He lay down
on the ground.
The fresh air
felt great.
Benito was in the U.S.!
For the time being,
he felt safe and sound.

## 4 Meeting Teresa

Benito Cruz
went to work
in the fields.
He moved
from farm to farm.
He picked
whatever vegetables
were in season.

Many of the other men
had families.
Benito spent
most of his off hours
with the single men.
Now and then,
they went to Los Angeles
to have a good time.

In his heart,
Benito wanted to have
a family of his own.
But he knew
he could not get married
while he was here.

To get married,
a person
had to have papers.
He would have to be legal.
Benito was not.

One night,
Benito was having a drink
at a bar
in the city.
He started talking
to a man
he did not know.

"I can get you
an American wife,"
the man told him.
"If you marry
an American,
you will get
a green card.
You will be legal.
You can live
in the U.S.
as long as you want."

This sounded
like a great idea
to Benito.
"How much
must I pay you?"
he asked the man.

"Only 800 dollars!"
said the man.
"I would like
to help you for nothing.
But I have costs.
Know what I mean?"

"For 800 dollars
I can be married *and* legal?"
asked Benito.

"Sure, you can,"
said the man.
"I will bring the girl
to this bar.
Come back here
next Friday night
at 8:00."

Benito came back
the next Friday.
He saw the man
across the dark room.
The man came over
with his hand out.
Benito passed 800 dollars
to the man.
Then the man
took Benito
to meet Teresa.

"Here she is,"
said the man.
"Meet Teresa Garcia."
Then he turned
and walked out the door.

Teresa and Benito
shook hands.
Benito liked
Teresa's face.
Her eyes
were large and brown.
Her long, black hair
was pulled back.

She wore
a pretty Mexican dress.
She looked
too good to be true.

Teresa also liked
what she saw.
She liked
Benito's warm eyes
and kind face.
And his smile.
She liked his smile.

"I am so happy
that you speak Spanish,"
Benito told her.
He took her hands
in his.
Then Benito and Teresa
sat down at a table.

Benito tried
to make small talk.
"When did you
become an American?"
he asked Teresa.
"Or were you born here?"

"Well, …"
Teresa began.
"I will tell you something.
But you must not tell
anyone else.
I bought a fake visa
to visit my aunt and uncle.
Tio found me work
in a dress factory.
Then I got sick.
Then I found work
at a different factory.
I have stayed here
much too long.
I am not legal.
I don't have
that magic paper."

"What?!"
cried Benito.
"That man said
you are American!
He said
that if I marry you
I could get my green card."

"I am sorry,"
said Teresa.
"I do not even know
that man.
He is a friend
of someone I work with.
They thought
that I should meet you.
That's all."

"I just lost
a lot of money!"
cried Benito.
"I'm a fool!"

With that,
he walked right out
of the bar.
He was too angry
for words.

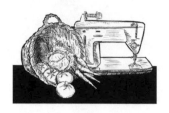

## 5 Looking for Her

The man from the bar
was long gone.
Benito knew
he would never find him.
He had to face the truth.
His money was gone.

But Benito
could not stop thinking
about Teresa Garcia.
She was not American.
She could not help him
get a green card.
But he couldn't get her
out of his mind.
He had to find her.
He had to see her again.

Night after night,
he went back
to the same bar.
He looked for Teresa
in the crowd.

"Do you know
Teresa Garcia?"
he asked people.
"She works in a factory."

Nobody knew her.
"Many, many factories
in L.A.,"
everyone said.
Night after night,
he went home
feeling down.

Benito could think
of only one thing to do.
He would have to find
Teresa's work place.
He rode the bus
all over Los Angeles.
Whenever he saw
a sewing factory,
he got off the bus.

He walked inside
each factory.
Every one of them
was noisy and hot.

"Is there a woman here
named Teresa Garcia?"
Benito asked over and over.

"No, sorry,"
he heard over and over.

But one day,
he heard
a different answer.

"Is there a woman here
named Teresa Garcia?"

"Who wants to know?"
said the woman
at the front desk.

"Benito Cruz."

"Do you work
for the government?"

"Of course not,"
said Benito.
"Teresa Garcia
is a friend of mine."

"Teresa Garcia
does not work here,"
said the woman.
"She did work here
not so long ago.
She left
when she got sick.
Maybe her friends
could help you out."

"Yes, I knew her,"
said one young woman.
"She lives
with her aunt and uncle
in East L.A."

"East L.A.
is a big place,"
said Benito.
"Do you know
which street?"

"Maybe 6th Street,"
said the woman.
"Near a park."

Benito headed
for East L.A.
He got off the bus
near the park.
He knocked
on every door.

"Do you know
a young woman
named Teresa Garcia?"
he asked everyone.

"No, sorry,"
was always the answer.

"I'll try
one more house,"
Benito said to himself.
He knocked
on the door.
A young woman
opened the door.
She had long, dark hair.
Benito knew her eyes
the second he saw her.
It was Teresa Garcia,
the one and only.

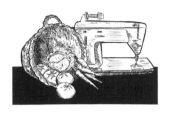

# 6  Making Plans

Benito told Teresa
how sorry he was
for walking out
of the bar.

But Teresa was happy
to see Benito.
She had
a big smile
on her face.
She couldn't believe
Benito had tried so hard
to find her.

"Now I have found you,"
said Benito.
"But what's next?"
I've lost 800 dollars
and a week of work.
I've got to get back
to the fields."

"Stay in Los Angeles,"
Teresa begged.

"Tio can get you a job
in a factory."

"Factory work?
I don't know,"
said Benito.
"I'm a country boy.
I like to be outside.
But I want to be
near you.
All right.
I'll try factory work.
Let's see
if your uncle
can find me a job."

And so Benito
started working
in a shirt factory.
Both he and Teresa
worked long days.
Benito found
a place to live
in East L.A.
It was easy
to see each other
after work.

"I want to marry you,"
Benito told Teresa
one night.

"Oh, Benito!
I want to marry you, too,"
Teresa said.
"But you know
we cannot be married
in the U.S.
Ncither of us
is legal."

"Let's go to Mexico,"
said Benito.
"We can marry there
and then come back
to California."

"I am so afraid
to cross the border again,"
said Teresa.
"And I want
my sister Raquel
to come up here."

"Then what will we do?"
Benito asked.

"We must go on
the way we are,"
said Teresa.
"We can still
see each other.
I will keep on working
at the dress factory.
You will keep on working
at the shirt factory.
But we cannot marry.
Not yet.
And we can't get caught.
We must be careful.
We must pay cash
for everything.
We cannot leave
a paper trail."

"What's a paper trail?"
Benito asked.

"Checks, bank records,
things like that,"
said Teresa.

"All those papers
make a trail.
They can follow the trail
to find us.
It would show
that we are not legal.
I don't want
to go back to Mexico
if you are here."

"I don't like
living like this,"
said Benito.

"What else
can we do?"
Teresa asked.
"We have more here
than back home."

That was all
that Teresa had to say
for that day.

# 7   Another Crossing

Every week,
Teresa sent a money order
to her family
in Mexico.
She kept a record
of all the money orders
she had sent.
She hid the paper
in her room.

A few years
went by.
Teresa had sent enough
to bring Raquel
to Los Angeles.

"All I need
is a visa,"
wrote Raquel.
"But getting a real visa
will take time.
We must wait
to see each other."

"Maybe Raquel
should buy a visa
the way I did,"
Teresa said to Benito.

"Don't you see?"
said Benito.
"Your visa
was not real.
You were never legal
in this country.
Not even for one day!
And a real visa
would not cost
so much money."

Teresa's head
was down.
"You are right,"
she said.
She turned her head up
and looked at Benito.
"I want my sister
to have real papers.
That will be
worth waiting for."

"Let's not fool ourselves,"
said Benito.
"She might never get
a visa.
She might never see
a better life.
She might die poor.
I think
we should go and get her!"

"I told you before,
I do not want
to cross the border.
Not now.
Not ever."

"Do you want
your sister
to be here?"
Benito asked.
"If you do,
then we must go
and get her.
And while we're in Mexico,
we can get married!"

"We could kill two birds
with one stone,"
said Teresa.
"I will think about
your idea."

Teresa told Tia
about Benito's idea.
"You are crazy kids!"
Silvia said.
"It would be nice
to bring Raquel here.
It would be nice
to get married.
Many things
would be nice.
But you must see things
for what they are.
You can get
back into Mexico.
Getting back
to the U.S.
is another story."

Tia said to wait.
She told Teresa
that a new law
might be coming.
The new law
would make it possible
to get a green card
and be legal.
"Then you can get married
right here in L.A.,"
she said.
"I love you, little one.
Sit back and wait
for luck to come your way."

"I love you too, Tia,"
said Teresa.
"But they will never pass
such a law!
It just won't happen."

A few days later,
she gave Benito
her answer.
"Let's go to Mexico,"
she said.

"We will get married.
Then we will bring Raquel
back to L.A.
We'll find a way."

Benito held her
in his arms.
"Yes, my angel,"
he said.
"We'll find a way."

Teresa did not tell
Tia or Tio
where she was going.
She told them
only that she was going
away.

Teresa and Benito
had no trouble
getting into Mexico.
That part of the trip
was easy.

# 8  Mexico City

Teresa and Benito
were on a bus
to Mexico City.
The bus stopped
along the way.
They got off
at a village.
They needed
something to eat.
They went
into a little place
along the road.
That is where
they heard the bad news.

"Mexico City
is a mess!"
they heard a man say.
"Many, many people
have lost their homes.
Many are dead.
They are still trying
to dig out the bodies.

Such bad luck!
An earthquake
right under the city!"

Teresa turned to Benito.
"An earthquake!
In Mexico City!
Oh, how I hope
my family is safe!"

They ate their food
in a hurry.
Then they caught
the next bus.

When they got
to Mexico City,
they could not
believe their eyes.
Buildings and homes
lay in pieces.
Rock and wood and glass
were everywhere.
It was hard to tell
where streets had been.
Children cried
for their mothers.

Mothers called
their children's names.
Red Cross workers
dug into the mess
to follow the cries.

   Teresa and Benito
somehow made their way
to Teresa's street.
She saw people
she knew.
"Have you seen anyone
from my family?"
she asked them.
They shook their heads.
It made Benito think about
when he was looking
for Teresa.

   And then Teresa
heard the answer
she did not want to hear.

   "Your whole family
was lost,"
an old woman told her.

"They are dead,
all of them.
I saw some men
carry away their bodies
just this morning."

"Raquel, too?"
Teresa asked.

"Yes, pretty girl,"
said the old woman.
Tears fell
from her eyes.

"Oh, Benito!"
cried Teresa.
"Why was I not here?
Why am I not dead too?"

Benito held her tight.
"Because you
are the lucky one,"
he said.
"You and I—
we are safe.

We can try
to go back
to Los Angeles.
Your sister Raquel
was not so lucky."

  Teresa did not feel safe.
But she took care
of matters
in Mexico City.
She found out
that her family
had been laid
in a huge grave
with many others.
She said goodbye
to what had been her home.
No one and nothing
was left for her here.
It was time
to head north again.

# 9  Back to L.A.

"Let's get married
before we leave,"
Benito said.

"I love you,"
said Teresa.
"But this is not
the right time.
I am too sad
about my family.
I want to be happy
on my wedding day.
And Mexico City
is in such bad shape.
I just want to go
back to L.A."

"Maybe you're right,"
said Benito.
"But what if this
is our only chance?
When will we
ever get married?"

"There will be
a right time,"
said Teresa.
"Please, let's leave now."

"Off we go!"
said Benito,
putting on a happy face.

They headed north.
They walked
along a road
until they got a ride.
When they got close
to the border,
the driver
dropped them off.
Benito and Teresa
sat down
by the side
of the road.
They waited
until it got dark.
Then they saw
a big truck
coming toward them.

"Here is our ride
across the border!"
said Benito.
He stepped out
to be in the truck's lights.
He waved his arms
in the air.
The truck stopped.
Benito handed money
to the driver.

"Get in the back!"
the driver shouted.

Benito and Teresa
walked behind the truck.
Benito knocked
on the back door.
Someone inside
pushed open the door.
Benito and Teresa
stepped up into the truck.

"See how easy?"
laughed Benito.
"We're almost there."

The truck
was hot and dark.
Teresa could not see faces.
But she could hear the
sounds
of many other people.
Some had bad colds.
Some made loud noises
in their sleep.
A bad smell
hung in the thick air.

"How soon
will we get out of here?"
she asked Benito.

"Not long,"
he whispered.

In a short while,
the truck stopped.
Benito and Teresa
heard someone banging
on the truck.

Suddenly,
the back door opened.

A man stood there.
Teresa and Benito
knew right away
who he was.
Words in a circle
on the man's shirt
spelled it out:
U.S. Border Patrol.

"Everyone out!"
the man shouted.

One by one,
40 people jumped
out of the truck.

"Stand over here!"
the man called out.
"In a line!
Everyone wait here.
Hurry up!"

"Where are we?"
Teresa asked.

Benito looked around.
"We're in California."

"We got caught
after we crossed?"
asked Teresa.

"I think so."

"Oh, I'm so afraid,"
said Teresa.

Benito put his arm
around her.
"Today we're not so lucky,"
he said.

## 10  Second Try

They didn't have to
stand in a line
for very long.
In just a few minutes,
a bus pulled up.

"Everyone on the bus!"
the Border Patrol shouted.
"Now!"

All the Mexicans
stepped up into the bus.
It was not
a large bus.
There were not enough seats
for everyone.
Some people
had to stand.

The bus
turned around
in the road.

It headed south,
back to Mexico.
The sun
was coming up.
Dawn was breaking.

Teresa saw
a little marker
along the road.
That must mean
we crossed the border,
she said to herself.
The land
looked the same
on both sides
of the marker.
All she could see
was sand and brush
all around.
About a mile
past the marker,
the bus stopped.

"Now, everyone out!"
shouted the Border Patrol.
"Go home!
And don't come back!"

The bus
made a loud noise
and pulled away.
A trail of dust
followed behind it.

The group waited
until the bus
was out of sight.
Then some of the people
began to walk
toward California.

Benito grabbed
Teresa's hand.
"Let's run!"
We're only a mile
from the border!"

"We are crazy kids,"
she laughed.
"Just like Tia said!"

She looked
at the land
in front of them.

"To me,
it all looks the same,"
she said.
"Mexico.
United States.
Why is this Mexico
and that the U.S.?"

    "Why were we born
poor in Mexico?"
said Benito.
"Why must we go
to all this trouble
to make a living?
Why can't we get married
in the United States?
Too many questions.
Too many things
to ask why about.
Things are as they are.
We do what we must."

    By the dawn's early light,
they crossed again.
But this time,
nobody stopped them.

# 11   A New Law

Back in Los Angeles,
Benito was not happy.
He did not like city life.
He hated factory work.

"I want to leave L.A.,"
he said to Teresa.
"I want to go and find
some farm work."

Teresa begged him
not to leave.
She told him
about a new law
that might be coming.
"Just think!"
she said.
"We could get
our green cards!
We could get married!
And then we'll find
better jobs!"

"If it becomes a law,
I will need
90 days of farm work
before May 1,"
said Benito.
"I can't wait around.
I must get to work
as soon as possible."

Benito and Teresa
held each other tight.
They could hardly breathe.

"Say we'll be together
sometime very soon,"
cried Teresa.

"I hope so,"
said Benito.
And he left
for the fields.

It was easy for him
to find farm work.
This time,
the work
was not close to L.A.

And life was not easy
for the workers.
They bent over
to pick vegetables.
All day long.
Day in and day out.
The sun beat down
on their backs.
When the sun went down,
they slept
on hard bunk beds
in one long building.
Or in a tiny house,
Or in a tent.
One after another,
the days were long
for Benito Cruz.

Then, in the fall,
the new law was passed.
Not everyone
liked the law.
But for people
like Teresa Garcia,
it was the best news ever.

She had lived
in the U.S.
since before 1982.
She would need a way
to show that.
She also would need
to pass a test
about American history
and government.
In English.
Then she would be legal.
After 18 months,
she could get
a green card.

The law
helped Benito, too.
He had done farm work
for 90 days
before May 1.
He, too,
could become legal.

But Teresa
did not know
where Benito was.
She had not seen him
for months.
She didn't know
if he had heard
about the new law.
She did not know
how to reach him.
All she could do
was wait
to hear from him.
She dreamed of him,
with hope in her heart.

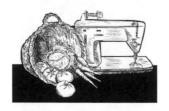

# 12   Waiting for Magic

"I'm going ahead
without Benito,"
Teresa told Silvia.
"I will try
to get my green card."

"Can you show
you have been here
since before 1982?"
her aunt asked.
"You have been so careful
not to leave
a paper trail."

"This is true,"
said Teresa.
"I have
no paper trail.
But I might have
one thing.
One little paper trail."

An office was set up
to help people
become legal.
Teresa went there
with her one paper.
The office
was very small.
It could hardly handle
the crowd of people.
"Get in line!"
a man shouted to Teresa.

Every person
in the long line
held a pile of papers.
Everyone wanted
to show how long
they had lived
in the U.S.
Teresa held
just one piece of paper.
She waited for her turn
to show it,
like everyone else.

At last,
it was Teresa's turn.

"This is all you have?"
the woman asked.
"Just one paper?
What is it?"

Teresa showed
her one paper.
It was a record
of all the money orders
she had sent
to her family
in Mexico.
On each line
was a date,
money order number,
and dollar amount.
The record began
in 1980.

"It is not much,"
said the woman.
"But it does go back
to before 1982.
We will let you know
if this is good enough."

Now Teresa
had two things
to wait for.
Benito was one.
A letter
from the U.S. government
was the other.
She might get
one of her wishes.
Or both.
Or nothing at all.
With all her heart,
she wanted both wishes.

One morning,
Teresa heard a knock
on the door.
She ran down the stairs
to answer it.

"You have mail!"
said Benito Cruz.

Teresa thought
she was dreaming!
There he was,
standing at the door!

She threw her arms
around Benito.
"Oh, you're here!"
she cried.

"And do you know
what else is here?
A letter
from the U.S. government!"
Benito waved it
in the air.

Teresa grabbed the letter
from his hand.
She tore it open.
Inside was the news
she had been waiting for.
The record
of her money orders
had won Teresa
her magic paper!

"You are next!"
she said to Benito.
"Can you show
that you worked
on a farm
for 90 days?"

Benito pulled a paper
out of his pocket.
It was a letter
from the farm company
that he worked for.
"This should do it!"
he said.
"We can get married
as soon as I get
my magic paper!"

"This paper
is worth its weight
in gold!"
cried Teresa.

"It is worth
more than gold!"
said Benito.
"It is worth the world
to you and me!"

"Yes, yes, it is!"
cried Teresa.
She held Benito
with all her might.

For the first time
in six years,
she felt safe.

The part of the law
that made people legal—
called amnesty—
ended after two years.
Teresa and Benito
were the lucky ones
who became legal
during that time.
At last,
they could get married,
and they did.

The story of Mexicans
coming to America
did not end there.
The story went on,
as Teresa and Benito
built a happy life.
They were legal.
They were safe.
They were together.
It felt like magic.

# Glossary

Definitions and examples of certain words and terms used in the story

---

**Chapter 1 – The Visa** page 1

**poked (to poke)** — To touch someone or something with a finger or stick.
*Then someone poked her.*

**take care of** — To help someone who is ill, disabled, or young.
*I want to take care of her.*

**whispered (to whisper)** — To speak very quietly.
*You will never get a visa here," he whispered.*

**turned down (to turn down)** — Not accepted.
*Many people are turned down.*

**fake** — Not legal; false.
*What if the fake visa didn't work?*

**work (to work)** — To be successful.
*What if the fake visa didn't work?*

**pulled into (to pull into)** — To arrive at.
*The bus pulled into Los Angeles.*

## Chapter 2 – Los Angeles page 5

**dirt poor** — Very poor.
*We are not dirt poor.*

**check (to check)** — To look at and inspect.
*No one there will check your visa.*

**piece work** — Not by the hour; payment for each product finished.
*It was piece work.*

**to run (runny nose)** — A condition in which "water" drips from the nose.
*Teresa's nose began to run.*

**better off** — In a better situation, usually financially.
*Her family back home would be better off.*

**green card** — A permit to live and work in the U.S.
*Both Tia and I have green cards.*

**papers** — Legal documents such as a green card.
*… lots of people live here without papers.*

## Chapter 3 – Benito page 11

**border** — The line that separates two countries. *You will get caught at the border.*

**fine** — Money paid for breaking a law.
*… a small fine for breaking the law.*

**coyote** — A guide who takes people across the border illegally.
*… he found a* coyote.

**Border Patrol** — Federal police who guard the U.S. border.
*Border Patrol all over.*

**wetbacks** — People who cross the border illegally.
*… a bus full of wetbacks.*

**pipe** — A large hollow tube.
*… a big pipe that went under ground.*

**crawl (to crawl)** — To move on hands and knees like a baby.
*Just crawl inside.*

**worm** — A small, snake-like animal that lives in the ground.
*Benito crawled along like a worm.*

**safe and sound** — Secure and not hurt.
*He felt safe and sound.*

---

## Chapter 4 – Meeting Teresa  page 19

**in season** — Vegetables (and fruit) that are ripe and ready for picking.
*… whatever vegetables were in season.*

**legal** — Lawful (illegal is against the law).
*He would have to be legal.*

**pulled back (to pull back)** — To tie or hold in place at the back of the head.
*Her long, black hair was pulled back.*

**a fool** — A person who makes a big mistake; a stupid person.
*I'm a fool!*

---

**Chapter 5 – Looking for Her** page 26

**feeling down** — Unhappy; depressed.
*He went home feeling down.*

**knocked (to knock)** — To hit something hard and quickly.
*He knocked on every door.*

---

**Chapter 6 – Making Plans** page 31

**paper trail** — A collection of receipts, payments, bills, and other things which show dates, times, and places.
*We cannot leave a paper trail.*

## Chapter 7 – Another Crossing  page 36

**money order** — A piece of paper that is like a bank check.
*Teresa sent a money order to her family.*

**hid (to hide)** — To put something in a secret place so nobody will find it.
*She hid the paper ...*

## Chapter 8 – Mexico City  page 42

**mess** — A situation where things are broken, destroyed, or not in good condition.
*Mexico City is a mess!*

**dig out (to dig out)** — To uncover something or someone that is buried.
*They are still trying to dig out the bodies.*

**earthquake** — A natural event; the ground shakes and may crack open.
*An earthquake right under the city.*

**Red Cross workers** — People who work for an organization that helps people.
*Red Cross workers dug into the mess.*

**bodies** — Dead people.
*They are still trying to dig out the bodies.*

**tears** — The "water" that comes from the eyes when a person cries.
*Tears fell from her eyes.*

**took care of (to take care of)** — To take action; to finish something.
*But she took care of matters.*

**matters** — Things such as business paper work and business papers.
*But she took care of matters.*

**found out (to find out)** — To learn; discover.
*She found out that her family ...*

**grave** — Hole in the ground for dead bodies.
*... in a huge grave with many others.*

---

**Chapter 9 – Mexico City** page 47

**dropped (them) off (to drop off)** — To leave someone or something somewhere.
*The driver dropped them off.*

---

**Chapter 10 – Second Try** page 53

**brush** — Plants, small trees, and bushes.
*All she could see was sand and brush.*

**pulled away (to pull away)** — To leave.
*The bus made a sound and pulled away.*

**to make a living** — To earn enough money to live well.
*Why go ... to all this trouble to make a living?*

---

**Chapter 11 – A New Law**  page 57

**passes (to pass)** — To be approved and become legal.
*If the law passes ...*

**bent over (to bend over)** — To lower one's back to be closer to the ground.
*They bent over to pick vegetables.*

**beat down (to beat down)** — To shine hard and hot on something or someone.
*The sun beat down on their backs.*

**bunk beds** — Two beds with one on top of the other.
*They slept on hard bunk beds.*

**tent** — A cloth or canvas shelter.
*They slept ... in a tent.*

---

**Chapter 12 – Waiting for Magic**  page 62

**handle (to handle)** — To manage; control.
*(The office) could hardly handle the crowd of people.*

**might** — Strength; very tightly.
*She held Benito with all her might.*

**amnesty** — A government pardon for people who may have broken a law.
*(The) amnesty ended after two years.*